THE STRAY AND THE STRANGERS

THE STRAY
AND THE
STRANGERS

Steven Heighton

Illustrations by Melissa Iwai

GROUNDWOOD BOOKS
HOUSE OF ANANSI PRESS
TORONTO BERKELEY

Groundwood Books / House of Anansi Press
groundwoodbooks.com

We gratefully acknowledge for their financial support of our publishing program the
Canada Council for the Arts, the Ontario Arts Council and the Government of Canada.

 Canada Council **Conseil des Arts**
for the Arts du Canada

 ONTARIO ARTS COUNCIL
CONSEIL DES ARTS DE L'ONTARIO
an Ontario government agency
un organisme du gouvernement de l'Ontario

With the participation of the Government of Canada
Avec la participation du gouvernement du Canada | Canadä

Library and Archives Canada Cataloguing in Publication
Title: The stray and the strangers / Steven Heighton ; illustrations by Melissa Iwai.
Names: Heighton, Steven, author. | Iwai, Melissa, illustrator.
Identifiers: Canadiana (print) 20190224711 | Canadiana (ebook) 20190225084 | ISBN
9781773063812 (hardcover) | ISBN 9781773063829 (EPUB) | ISBN 9781773063836 (Kindle)
Classification: LCC PS8565.E451 S77 2020 | DDC jC813/.54—dc23

Jacket and interior illustrations by Melissa Iwai
Jacket design by Michael Solomon
Map by Mary Rostad and Steven Heighton

Groundwood Books is committed to protecting our natural environment. This book is
made of material from well-managed FSC®-certified forests, recycled materials, and
other controlled sources.

Printed and bound in Canada

MIX
Paper from
responsible sources
FSC® C016245

For the thousands of children
who passed through the OXY transit
camp on Lesvos in 2015

1
Boat Strangers

The steep, narrow streets of the island town swarmed with stray dogs, and almost all of them looked alike. They were middle-sized, spotted brown on gray, and they had sharp, alert-looking ears.

There was one exception. She was smaller and scrawnier than the others. Her whole pelt was the color of cinnamon except for her paws, which were white, as if she were wearing socks. Her long brown ears drooped like vine leaves wilted at the end of summer.

An old fisherman was the first to call her Kanella, the Greek word for cinnamon.

"She must have come here as a stowaway on one of your boats," he teased the younger men. "You never seem to know what you've got aboard."

In the harbor, the fishermen would sort their catch and fling the smaller unwanted fish onto the pier. Kanella waited there each day beside a mob of stout, cantankerous cats. She lay flat on her empty belly, half hidden behind coils of rope or piles of netting that smelled of brine and seaweed. Whenever she tried to creep closer, the cats would hiss like vipers.

The old man chuckled as the young ones tried to tease him back.

"We know the dog arrived on your boat, old man!"

"That's right. They say you found her in your nets with the bass."

"No, with the shrimp! She isn't much bigger."

"The old man's eyes are too weak to see the difference."

"Or maybe she swam here from Turkey," said another, pointing across the water to a mountainous shore. "The eels wouldn't bother to eat her, skinny as she is."

"You think she's strong enough to swim that far?"

"Why don't we throw her in and find out?"

The fishermen went on laughing and tossing scraps at the strays. As the cats pounced, shrieking quarrels would erupt. If a fish head or tiny squid slapped down near Kanella, she would dart out, sweep it up in her jaws and flee.

The fishermen cheered and chanted her name whenever she managed this feat.

"Look, the runt has done it again! Clever girl."

"If she's so clever, why doesn't she find food at the dump like the other dogs?"

"I hear the others chase her away."

She knew only a few of the words, but she understood the tone: cheerful and good-hearted. Still, she never approached the men or let them touch her. To her, all the townspeople were frightening giants, even the children.

As for the island's summer visitors, they were even bigger and louder. They would loom and lumber toward her, trying to pat her or scoop her up in their arms — an insult, as if she were a mere puppy.

When her stomach ached a little less, she would trot uphill through a labyrinth of cobblestone lanes and stairways to the top of the town. There she slept in a hollow in the trunk of an olive tree that grew by the wall of a ruined castle. This had been her home for two hot, dry summers and rainy winters — as far back as she could remember.

Other strays never climbed up here. It was too far above the harbor where the boats came in, too far from the dump, too far from the restaurants that threw out so much food in the busy summers.

Her burrow was safe, but in the winter it was cold.

And all year round it was lonely.

~~~~~~~~

One day the boats returned to the harbor early, riding low in the water as if they were loaded with a heavy catch. Yet Kanella's twitching nose caught no scent of fish.

The decks of the boats were crowded with strangers. They looked and sounded nothing like the people of the town. Many wore bright orange vests over ragged clothing that was sopping wet, as if the fishermen had hauled them out of the sea. Dark scarves covered the hair of the women. The children shivered the way Kanella did every winter, when the winds carved the sea into steep, frothing waves and the boats huddled in the harbor for days.

The fishermen helped the strangers climb down onto the pier, where they stood or sat in trembling clusters. The old fisherman called in a shaking voice to people at the restaurants along the pier,

"Come help us! They are cold and hungry. We need a doctor!"

Soon people emerged from the restaurants with water and platters of food. But some of the strangers seemed too ill and weary to eat. Kanella watched hungrily as the bolder dogs and cats darted in among their wet shoes to seize fallen bits of bread, cheese or fish. The animals worked quickly, afraid of being kicked or chased.

Yet it was the strangers who flinched and backed away, as if they were the ones who should be frightened.

~~~~~~~~

As the spring sun climbed higher and grew hotter, more and more strangers arrived on the island. Some continued to come on the fishing boats. Others appeared, sodden and silent, up on the olive-green decks of coast-guard ships. But most of them landed in black rubber rafts so crammed with passengers that they seemed more under water than above.

Kanella's sharp eyes would spot the rafts crawling across the sea as she stood outside her burrow above the town. Then she would hurry down to the harbor. She was hoping to find scraps of food left on the pier, but she was also curious. Where did the strangers come from? They shrank away from cats and dogs, so they scared her a little less than the towns-people did.

Wherever they came from, they were wary, tired and thin.

Strangers of another kind were arriving now, too. They came not over the sea but along the highway in cars and buses. Many of them looked and sounded like the summer tourists — yet these people didn't climb up to visit the castle or swim in the sea. They walked fast and spoke urgently. Day and night they were in the harbor, bringing blankets, dry clothes and food to the boat strangers.

Sometimes they helped carry sick people off the rafts onto the pier. The sick people would lie under blankets while helpers knelt beside them or rushed around them, pointing and hollering.

Kanella knew what it meant to be so hungry and tired that you could hardly stand up. Still, she did not move in to take the scraps that the helpers sometimes fed to the other dogs. Then one day she saw one of the rescued children give a piece of cheese to a cat. The child did not seem afraid, even when her parents pulled her back and scolded her.

Kanella could almost imagine accepting food from a hand that small.

2
The Bearded Man

One morning, some helpers led a crowd of boat strangers through the white-walled streets of the town, then along the highway cut into the face of the cliffs. Kanella followed, keeping her distance. The sea swayed and shimmered far below. Cars and trucks snarled and rattled past.

The large group came to a wide, bare lot beside the road.

Last summer, cars would park here in rows. Tourists would drink, dance and yell at the moon from the balcony of a building that shook with drumbeats and shone with light. Sometimes Kanella found tasty scraps in the dark behind the building — nuts, salty olives, oily strips of fried potato that looked like fingers.

But at summer's end, the building fell dark and silent. It remained that way now.

Maybe the town no longer had room for tourists, with so many boat strangers landing?

In the bare lot beside the building, two huge tents had sprung up. Around them were smaller tents and huts. Kanella ran around the edges of the camp, her nose skimming the ground. Everything smelled new, even the toilet shed with its harsh chemical scent.

From a distance, she tried to see into the giant tents. Many boat strangers sat inside, eating or quietly talking. Behind them, others lay wrapped in blankets on mats.

Never before had she seen people sleeping on the ground, like her.

One of the huts gave off rich, mingled aromas of food. Was it a sort of restaurant, like the ones along the pier? If so, a dog would not be welcome, but scraps might be found around the back — maybe potato fingers, fish bones or bread crusts.

A man came out the door. He had a beard like some of the fishermen, and he looked older than the other helpers. He held Kanella's gaze. Then he waved to her and displayed his teeth.

Was this a welcoming grin, or a warning?

He ducked back into the shelter, then reappeared. He came toward her, limping a little.

"Here, come on," he said. "It's all right."

Kanella backed away. He stopped and lowered himself awkwardly to one knee, as if trying to make himself small. His eyes were clear and pale as water.

When he held out his open hand, she smelled and saw something on it. Cheese of some kind? She wished he would just fling it. But he kept holding it out and beckoning with his odd-sounding words.

"That's it. Come. We can be friends."

She crept forward, too hungry to resist.
She lipped the food quickly. Then she
backed off and bolted it — a flat, smooth
shred of cheese without flavor, unlike any
she had ever known.

"There. You see?"

The man's scent was strong and smoky
but not unpleasant.

Again he edged forward, stretching out
his empty hand. Again she withdrew.

The man stood up. Once more his teeth
showed in his beard.

"All right. I understand. Real friend-
ships take time."

He limped back to the food hut, glanc-
ing at her over his shoulder. She wanted to
follow. She didn't move.

He vanished into the doorway. But soon after, a hand appeared there holding a bowl.

The hand set the bowl down outside the door and withdrew.

The door eased shut.

On silent paws she snuck up and sniffed. Late spring was always a thirsty time. The sun had dried up the last winter rainpools and most of the streams.

Fixing her eyes on the door, she lapped up the water and licked the bowl dry.

3
The Camp

The next day, Kanella trailed an even larger group of boat strangers as they trudged up the road from the harbor. When they arrived at the camp, they formed a long and silent line outside the food hut. Through an opening in the wall, helpers handed out bottles of water, bowls of food and slices of bread.

Face-to-face through the slot, the strangers and the helpers spoke to each other, not with words but with their eyes, hands and sometimes smiles.

The water bowl sat on the ground by the closed door of the hut. The bowl was full again, but Kanella was wary of going closer with so many people milling around.

Doors were a mystery. The many doors of the town were forever enticing her with the heavy scent of food — so she would sniff the air and edge closer. Usually the doors stayed shut. But sometimes they would burst open like great toothless mouths and people would spill out. A few had even yelled and kicked at her.

Now the door of the food hut opened. Kanella leapt back. The bearded man stood there. He knelt with a puff of breath and pointed at the water bowl.

"Come now. You must be thirsty."

His fingers, holding something, reached toward her. She sniffed — another piece of cheese. She edged forward and pinched it from his grip.

He reached out to touch her head. There were gray hairs in his beard below his mouth, like on the muzzle of an old dog.

He scratched her ears.

"You're not so shy now. And why should you be? We're all friends here."

She didn't understand him, but his words, like his hand, were calm and kind. She stood very still, her heart thumping in her throat.

A younger helper, her face so dark it was almost black, appeared in the doorway beside the man. Crouching lightly, this woman offered a piece of cold meat. It was thin, flat and bland, like the cheese.

"You'll like this even better," she said. Her voice was higher and thinner than the man's, but just as kind.

Kanella wolfed the meat down with a gulp. The belch that followed was louder still.

The man and woman laughed.

And Kanella let the woman stroke her head.

~~~~~~~~

At sunset a few days later, instead of leaving and trotting back to town, Kanella curled up to sleep beside the water bowl and the food-hut door.

The evening after that, the man invited

her into the hut with his hands and his words.

"You can sleep in here, girl. It's going to be a windy night."

Never had she passed through the mouth of a door into a human space. It was warm, and like her burrow in the tree it kept out the sky.

The man pointed to a gray blanket on the ground under a table. It was a dim place, a den within a den. Kanella curled up there and closed her eyes, though behind her heavy eyelids a part of her stayed awake and watchful.

Her new den was a good spot to pass the hot hours of spring's warmest days. But even in the heat, the food hut was a busy place.

Nights were quieter. The bearded man, the young woman or one of the others would sleep there on a narrow bed that was like a long chair. Sometimes the sleeper would have to rise, unshutter the slot in the wall and pass drinks or bowls of food to a new group of strangers.

Other times, helpers in white aprons stained with food would enter, bearing heavy pots or trays. Kanella knew this food came from a truck trailer by the road. It smelled like a restaurant, and smoke was always flowing from its chimney.

~~~~~~~

Everything about the boat strangers mystified Kanella. But the oddest thing was that they didn't remain in the camp that they had taken such trouble to reach. Here there was shade, water, plenty to eat and friendly people. Yet early each morning the strangers who had arrived the day before would set off. They would plod and limp up the sticky black road that looped along the sea.

Kanella had never known people to move so wearily and yet walk so far. How did the children do it? Adults carried the smallest, but the others walked by themselves, their short legs churning to keep up. With her eyes she could follow them all for hours, a straggling line crawling along the cliffs in the distance.

One morning, curiosity pushed her to

follow a departing group. She padded quietly behind them. In her mind she was one of the helpers now. She would keep the group moving and together.

And so she did. When the lagging adults and children glanced back and saw her slinking along, they looked alarmed and sped up.

Once she realized how much she was helping, she puffed up a little and allowed herself a few instructive barks. *This way! Everyone together. Keep to the side. A truck is coming!*

She followed them until the sun was high and the road smelled of tar and stuck to her pads.

Every morning after, she did the same,

following until thirst and hunger made her turn back. And every noon as she returned, running at full stretch, the camp helpers would welcome her: "Kanella, Kanella, Kanella!"

4
Summer

In the fiery heat of summer afternoons, Kanella rested in her cool den under the table. The man now wore a hat. It smelled like sweet grass and cast a shadow on his red face. His eyes seemed bluer than ever.

The young woman and some others now wore dark glasses that hid their eyes in a way that made Kanella uneasy. But they continued to treat her fondly and give her so much to eat that her stomach ached, though in a different way than before.

"Here, girl. Try what's left," the young woman said. "My lunch from town." The little cubes of spicy meat wrapped in bread were delicious, mostly. Kanella spat out some bitter, crunchy strips that burned her tongue.

"Oh, you wanted yours without onion? Getting particular, I see." The woman's eyes were hidden, but the words sounded kind. "If only you were that fussy about having a bath now and then. You don't smell as sweet as your name."

~~~~~~

The boat strangers kept arriving. They were wet, shivering and caped in blankets, in spite of the heat. The big sleeping tents were always full now. Some people had to lie outside on blankets on the ground.

Inside or out, they slept poorly, especially the children. Their piercing cries and strangled gasps startled Kanella awake.

These sounds rarely woke whichever helper was in the food hut. People, she was learning, had very weak ears. So she would have to push the door open with her nose and squirm through. Usually by the time she got outside, the frightened sleeper had gone quiet.

One morning, some new children were playing in front of the big tents. Their parents, slumped on benches, watched them. They had removed their shoes and turned them upside down to drain water out of them, then set them in the sun to dry.

The children were kicking a ball around with the bearded man and a few other helpers. The bearded man ran stiffly, a hitch in his stride. Yet his feet on the ball were as nimble as mice. The children thronged around him like puppies.

Kanella hesitated. Then, unable to resist, she dashed in among those churning legs. The children passed the ball around her while she yelped and gave chase.

Again she noticed how the boat children never tried to touch her the way tourist children did. These children gave off a slight smell of fear, like the scent of a wet coin between cobblestones. As they swarmed close to her, their laughter grew shrill.

Finally, she pounced on the ball and bit down. It collapsed between her paws with a sigh.

The bearded man laughed. Then he knelt down and gently pried the shrunken thing from her mouth. Some of the children laughed, too, but their laughter was uneasy and they kept their distance.

"Alas, my girl, you have caught and killed our only ball. I will have to go fix it. Next time, I hope you'll play more gently."

~~~~~~

The sun was peaking lower in the sky each noon. Yet it still left the black road sticky and the brown earth hard and dry. Kanella knew all of the camp helpers now by their smell, voice, face, walk, the different weight of their fingers on her head.

Sometimes instead of water, they filled her bowl with the best thing she had ever tasted. *Milch*, the bearded man called it, and the young woman used a similar sound, *milk*. While Kanella slurped it up, the man would crouch beside her.

She no longer worried that he might snatch the bowl away at any time. On the contrary, she trusted that he and the young woman would keep filling it.

~~~~~~~~

One cool, sunny morning, she crept to the

edge of a ball-kicking game and tried to catch the bearded man's eye. He met her gaze and nodded. She rushed in and gave chase. When she managed to capture the ball, she resisted the urge to pounce, bite and shake it to death.

This morning there was a new boy. He was one of the smallest players and certainly the thinnest. Under his dark eyes there were shadows. Bones pushed out against the brown skin of his face.

As Kanella surged among the shrieking children, he let her come close and even brush against him. Then he ran his hand along her back, which she liked.

But he grew bolder. He gripped her tail and squeezed. This startled and offended her. She flashed her teeth at him, growling softly. The boy flinched. But then he smiled with gapped teeth and came at her again.

"Kanella, *no!*" the bearded man rumbled. He pointed toward the food hut.

She skulked away. The tail the boy had grabbed was curled between her legs.

She was confused. What had she done wrong? Could the man not see that the boy was being rude? Then again, the boy was small and very young. He would learn better manners, and she could help teach him.

The next sunrise, the many strangers who had arrived the day before set out along the road. But this time one of them stayed behind: the boy. He stood between the young woman and the bearded man, whose large hand enclosed the boy's.

The man and woman smelled of worry. Kanella was troubled, too. She wanted to herd that group of strangers, but she also wanted to stay close to the child.

Why had the group left him behind? Where was his family?

She stood on the edge of the road, looking back and forth between the departing strangers and the boy.

The boy said something she didn't understand. Then he said it louder.

It was her name, though strangely voiced, as if he were clearing his throat with the word. Still, he was calling her, and she went to him.

5
The Boy

The winds grew colder and the seas rougher. Yet the strangers kept arriving until the camp could barely hold them. The lineups outside the food hut grew longer by the day. Many of the children, holding their parents' hands, cried as they waited.

Each morning, another crowd of weary people would trek away up the road. Yet the boy remained, and Kanella stayed close beside him. Until now she had never had time to grow familiar with any boat stranger's face, voice or smell.

The boy's smell was like the scent of the baking bread that used to wake her in her burrow as it wafted up from the town. His clothes, though long since dry, still smelled of the sea.

The helpers brought the boy food and played with him. They made a bed for him in the food hut. He slept between Kanella's table and a metal box that glowed and hummed and breathed out heat.

Pointing and shaking their heads, the helpers made it clear to the boy that he should stop giving half of his food to Kanella. The bearded man scolded them both, though he smiled on one side of his beard as he did so.

"Do we not give you enough, my girl? Ah, I see by your face. You know we do. In fact, I see by your belly. You're not a wisp of a thing anymore."

She wagged her tail and made a sound in her throat to show she was listening. The boy imitated the sound — it was rather a poor imitation, she felt — and nodded.

"We're still hoping to find this one's parents, you see. And if we do, we want him to be as healthy and well fed as you."

Kanella wagged her tail, and again the boy grabbed it, laughing. He couldn't help himself, it seemed.

She pulled away. But this time she didn't growl, and the bearded man patted and praised her.

~~~~~~~~~~

At times after the boy went to sleep, curled under piled blankets, helpers would gather in the food hut. They would sit around the droning stove, drink tea and talk.

Kanella liked the hut to be packed and cozy this way, but more and more now the voices sounded uneasy. Often the helpers nodded toward the boy while they talked. Kanella watched through half-open eyes as she lay in her den or, at times, on the ground beside his cot.

One night, the sleeping boy began to whimper and thrash. He threw out his arms as if fending off danger.

The helpers fell silent. He kept repeating the same sounds, *baba* and *mama*.

The young woman stood up. Kanella was on her feet now, too, the hairs of her ruff hackling. She sniffed the boy's face and licked his cheek. He continued to squirm. Out of the corner of her eye, she saw the helpers watching.

She hopped up onto the cot beside the boy, then glanced at the young woman, who said, "Good girl, Kanella!"

She lay down beside the boy and burrowed her nose beneath the layers of wool. The boy's panting breaths began to slow. Still asleep, he draped an arm over Kanella's back.

With her head under the blankets, she couldn't see the helpers, but she heard them talking again in that uneasy tone. Several times she heard her own name.

"If they send him to the big camp, I doubt there will be a Kanella there to comfort him."

"In Mordor? Fat chance. No comfort there for love or money."

"Maybe we'll be able to keep him here till we find his parents."

"Looks like Kanella hopes so, too. Don't you, girl?"

Despite the voices, Kanella drifted toward sleep. The warmth of the boy and the blankets revived a good memory of lying in her old burrow, nestled against the other pups and the enormous body of her mother.

~~~~~~~~

When she was beside the boy he always slept deeply, until long after sunrise. If she wanted to play — and she always did — she had to prod his chest with her paw, then lick his face until his dark eyes opened. He would show the gaps between his teeth and reach out to tug her ears.

She did not love having her ears tugged but decided to tolerate this small liberty.

In the early light, before the camp filled up again, they would play the ball game.

The boy would dance over and around the spinning, skidding ball, somehow keeping it away from her.

But she was improving. She had learned to fake with her head and swipe with her paws. And when she managed to nab the ball, she would race away, rolling it ahead of her with her nose while he ran laughing behind her.

She had learned not to spoil the game by biting the ball to death. And he had learned not to grab her tail — at least not as often or as hard.

6
Winter

First came icy rains, then a few sharp-sided flakes of snow that Kanella caught on her tongue. They were wet and fresh like rain but gritty like sand.

The days seemed too cold now for journeys. Yet the strangers kept coming across the water. In the huge tents they huddled even closer, under coats and blankets, around stoves like the one in the food hut.

They no longer had to cross the island on foot. Instead they formed lines and waited until reeking buses shuddered into the camp. The tired strangers climbed aboard and looked out the windows as the doors closed with a huff and the machines groaned away. Some of the strangers waved at Kanella and the boy, who liked to watch the buses come and go.

Whenever a new group of strangers arrived, the bearded man would hurry the boy out to meet them. Sometimes the sun had barely risen. Kanella would try to follow, but the bearded man made her wait inside. Through a crack in the door she would listen and watch, hoping the boy would soon return to his cot. Everyone would be talking quickly, shaking their heads and looking worried.

In the end, the boy always seemed disappointed.

The buses were not the only change. Tall people who spoke loudly and walked with a heavy tread now came to the camp. They arrived in large white cars with markings on the side. Those same markings appeared on the front of their coats. They were constantly writing things down or pressing their hands to their cheeks and talking to no one.

Whenever they showed up, the helpers shut Kanella in the food hut with the boy and told her to stay put. Again she would spy through a crack in the door as the loud visitors spoke to the bearded man, the young woman and the other helpers.

Once, the bearded man returned to the hut, took the boy by the hand and led him out the door. He signaled Kanella to sit and stay. Then he put his finger up to his beard and said, "Hush!"

Outside, the man kept his arm around the boy's tiny shoulders. One of the visiting men pointed at the boy and spoke firmly. This other man, too, was bearded, though his beard was orange, his eyes were cold green and he was very tall.

Kanella growled softly. The tall man squinted over at the food hut, as if trying to see through the crack in the door. The bearded man moved to block his view. He put a hand on the tall man's shoulder and steered him away.

The young woman glanced at the hut with wide eyes and set a finger to her lips.

~~~~~~~~

A few mornings later, with no warning, the tall man burst into the food hut where Kanella was curled up with the boy. The young woman, who had been up serving food for much of the night, lay asleep, breathing heavily, on the other cot.

Kanella leapt down and faced the man, rumbling her guard-growl. Her heart was thudding.

The man's cold eyes rounded. He aimed a finger at Kanella.

"You can't have a dog in a food facility!" he said sharply. "And it shouldn't be anywhere near the boy! It shouldn't be in here at all!"

Kanella peeled back her lips, showing her fangs. She was trembling with rage. The skin along her spine was icy cold. Through all of the commotion, the boy and the exhausted woman remained asleep.

The man's red face grew redder as he shrank back. Seeing her water bowl in the corner, he kicked it over.

Then he pulled the door shut with a crash.

7
A Kind of Miracle

That night, the first heavy snow fell. Kanella curled beside the boy under their layers of wool. He was asleep. She lay listening, peeking out.

Never had the hut been so crammed with helpers sitting around the stove. Again they were speaking in that worried tone she disliked. Earlier, the bearded man had brought in a pine tree and stood it in the corner. He and the boy had draped its branches with shiny objects — spoons, tin-

foil birds, a belt buckle, copper buttons —
and strings of small puffed nuggets that
Kanella had discreetly nibbled off.

Now the worried talk went on while the
boy's breathing settled. Again she heard
her name among the words. Were they angry at her about the tree? She tried to stay
alert, but she had eaten so much tonight
and they had given her an extra bowl of
milk. And the crowded hut was so warm.

She fell into a heavy, dreamless sleep.

~~~~~~~~~

When she woke up, feeling cold, the boy
was gone, the hut empty. She struggled
out from under the blankets, nosed open
the door and ran outside.

In the early morning light, two boat strangers were kneeling and clasping the boy tightly as if to crush him. The boy was crying. The bearded man, the young woman and some other helpers just stood watching while these strangers attacked the boy!

Kanella barked fiercely, lowered her head and charged, laying back her ears, snarling as she ran.

The bearded man blocked her path. Stretching his arms wide, he roared, *"Kanella!"*

She tried to dart between his legs, but his hand flashed down and firmly gripped her ruff. She squealed, trying to twist free. Desperate, she nipped his hand. He gasped in pain and cuffed her nose.

The blow wasn't hard, but the shock of it made her yelp and freeze.

The man crouched down, pulled her close and stroked her head.

"Ah, Kanella, forgive me. Our tempers are all so short now, even yours. But look! Something wonderful has happened. A kind of miracle."

She peered around him. The strangers — a man and a woman — were still squeezing the boy. Their faces were as wet as if they had just been plucked from the sea. Their eyes, though red, were alive with joy.

The boy was not trying to escape them. He was clinging to them as tightly as they were holding him.

The faces of the helpers, too, shone wetly.

Now the bearded man released Kanella. She ran over to join the boy. The man and the woman flinched, but the boy pulled her — up on her hind legs now — into his arms.

"Khanella!" he said. Then he added words that the young woman often recited. "She is a good dog, but she needs a bath."

The strangers regarded her less fearfully now. They spoke to the boy in their throaty language. She licked the boy's face and seemed to taste the sea that had brought him to her island.

~~~~~~~

All too soon the boy and the two boat strangers, along with many others, were climbing aboard a rumbling bus. Kanella stood beside the bearded man, who was kneeling and gripping her by the ruff.

"You stay here with us, Kanella. This is your home, for now. He and his family have to travel on and find one for themselves."

With panicked eyes she watched the bus door close. Why was the bearded man allowing the boy to leave the camp? The boy's round face appeared in a square window, the woman's face behind his. As she waved, she smiled, but the boy did not.

A frantic squeal burst up out of Kanella's chest. She wrenched herself free and sprinted after the bus as it pulled out onto the road.

"Kanella, stop! Come back!" yelled the bearded man.

At first she was catching the bus, closer and closer. She breathed in its dirty brown breath as she gazed up, hoping to see a window and a face looking out.

The bus was speeding up, snarling back at her. She ran after it with all her heart. But it was pulling away. She tried to run faster, yet fell farther behind.

For a long time she kept trying, following from a distance until she could barely see it, hoping it might tire out and slow down.

When she could no longer even hear the bus, she stopped and stood panting in the middle of the road.

At last she turned and walked slowly back toward the camp. By the time she got there, the sun was low in the sky. The bearded man was sitting outside by the door of the food hut. She could see his breath.

As she approached, he stood stiffly. His eyes were sad but his teeth showed in his beard. He held the door open for her.

"It does my heart good to know we haven't lost you, too," he said.

8
Orphan

Some boat strangers arrived the next morning. But it was only a small group. There were no children among them.

That same evening, the small group departed on a single half-sized bus. No one arrived to replace them.

Silent helpers and people from the town piled up mats and blankets. They began to take down the huge tents. The silver trailer that always smelled of hot food was hauled away by a truck.

Everyone moved with a drooping slowness — shoulders slumped, feet heavy. Yet somehow the work went fast.

The camp was vanishing before Kanella's eyes.

A stinging snow whipped in off the sea as she ran around the site. A few helpers were fighting the wind to pick up diapers, plastic cups and water bottles, stuffing them into bags. She barked at them to stop. But they ignored her, as if the wind were swallowing her sounds.

No one would meet her gaze or speak to her.

She trudged back to the food hut and nosed the door open.

The young woman was gone. The stove

was gone. All that remained of the pine tree were some faded needles in the dirt. The table that had roofed her den was gone, too, though her blanket still lay on the ground.

No smell of food. Her water bowl empty.

The bearded man came into the hut. As he gazed at Kanella, the blue of his eyes deepened and softened.

"Ah, my poor girl. Now you are going to be an orphan, too."

The man took a last box of the milk Kanella loved. He knelt beside her in his tottery way, like on the first day when he had fed her. There were more white hairs in his beard. He filled her bowl with the milk, but she ignored it. She leaned against his leg, pushing her head deeper into his warm palm.

~~~~~~~~

At first light the next morning, she woke, cold, on her blanket.

How she missed the warmth and smell of the boy. The man was sleeping on his own cot under a heap of blankets. His ragged breaths were misting the cold air of the hut.

She nudged open the door.

Nothing remained of the camp. It had turned back into a big, empty parking lot.

She decided to venture down the road to the town. Perhaps more boat strangers were arriving there. If she could lead a large group of them back here, the camp might start to fill up again.

She started down the road, then heard the door of the hut open behind her.

The bearded man was calling her name. How breathless and small his voice sounded!

The faster and farther she ran, the fainter his voice. She had never ignored him this way before, but she had to do it. He would understand when she returned with more strangers, who would need him and the whole camp again.

The mountains still hid the rising sun, but up ahead its honey-colored light was spilling across the water. She reached the town and loped up through its silent lanes to her old burrow in the olive tree. From this high point, she peered out to sea.

Just as she had hoped — more boats and rafts were coming in!

She pelted down through the maze of streets to the harbor. Only a few towns-people were out. They leapt aside to let her pass. Despite her cinnamon fur and white socks, no one recognized her. She didn't slink along now, skittish and guarded. She moved with purpose.

In the harbor, dozens of dejected cats watched as fishermen helped dripping strangers onto the pier. Kanella streaked among them, barking frantically. She started up the road and then glanced back, trying to make the strangers understand.

This way! Follow me!

They were being led toward a row of buses by the tall people who wore matching coats, strode with loud steps and talked brusquely. She followed the group, repeating her message. But over the sound of tramping feet, shouting adults and crying children, no one seemed to hear.

The buses swallowed up the strangers and rumbled away as Kanella nipped at their wheels and ran in front of them. Their engines and blaring horns drowned out her barking.

There were too many buses to chase, and she knew now that she couldn't catch them.

She trotted back up the road. Maybe a few boat strangers had found their way to the camp without her. She had not felt this empty and hungry since first finding a home in the food hut.

She reached the flat, wide place where the camp had been. Even the food hut was gone. Cold winds moaned across the bare lot. She sniffed the ground and caught traces of familiar scents. The man and the young woman. The pine tree. Milk.

Those good smells made a clear trail that she followed straight to her bowl and blanket, still there on the ground.

The bowl was full of milk. Heavy stones sat on the corners of the blanket so the wind couldn't blow it away.

The milk was very cold and thick. She drank it before it could harden.

Then she curled into a ball on the blanket and scarved her tail over her nose.

9
Going North

She woke quivering with cold. It was night, and it seemed that the wind was howling and the moon was shining.

She raised her head and saw *two* moons.

They were the burning eyes of a small car. The howling was the car's engine.

Something was moving toward her, a shadow against the white lights. Was it the loud, angry official?

She did not rise, bark or even whimper.

Then she caught a familiar scent. The bearded man. On trembling legs she stood to greet him, her whole body wagging.

He crouched on one knee and buried his face in her ruff. She heard her name among his words.

"I thought I had to leave you, Kanella, but now I find I can't."

Licking his face, she tasted saltwater, like on the face of the boy just before he left. That taste and memory filled her with yearning and panic, but now the man was gathering her in his arms and carrying her to the car.

"Who knows how I'll get you home across so many borders? Come, my little stowaway."

He set her in the back, and moments later they were moving.

Kanella had never been inside a car. Beyond the window, stars drifted like faraway rafts over the black sea of the sky. The car's warmth and humming and the scent of the man calmed her and she fell back to sleep.

For two nights and days, she traveled in this new den.

In a line of other cars, they drove clattering into the dark belly of a ship that stank of oily fuel and steel. Alone she waited while the ship groaned, juddered and rolled, but she wasn't afraid. The man's smell and presence were strong in here. She knew he would come back. When he did, they drove out of the ship onto a huge pier and journeyed on in the morning light.

At times she watched his hands holding the wheel or met his red eyes in the mirror. Mostly, she slept.

Each time she hopped down out of the car, the snow was deeper, the air colder, the smells foreign. Never had she sniffed air that lacked the salt tang of the sea. Never had she felt a sun so pale and weak, or seen so many trees stripped bare as if dead.

Kanella woke in the dark as the car slowed down. Was she dreaming? Slowly they passed a long line of boat strangers who were waiting in front of a gate blocked by men in uniform. Whining, she put her paws up on the window. She searched for the boy's face in that line of cold, tired faces.

The man reached back to pat her, then firmly forced her down.

"Hush, girl. Go back to sleep. We still have a long way to go."

As she burrowed back under her blanket, he said softly, "Though not as far as they do."

Later she woke in the dark again. His sleeping head was next to hers, his seat stretched back like the cot in the food hut. The sound of his breathing was like winter waves on the shores of her island.

She knew that the island lay far behind them now.

At last he was calling her name, waking her from a deep sleep. He lifted her up and set her down in snow that came up to her chest. He pointed to a house.

It was not made of stone, like the white houses of the island, but of dark wood. Tall pines grew around it. Sweet-scented smoke rose in a bushy plume.

She waddled after him through the snow, trying to step in his tracks.

At the door he said her name in the voice she loved and invited her inside.

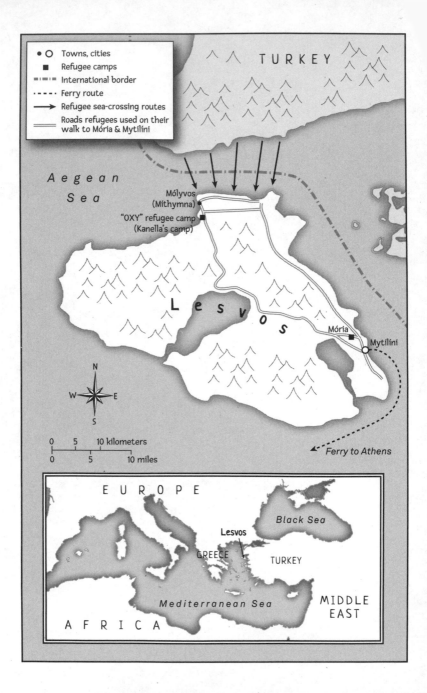

AFTERWORD

Since 2015, over a million refugees and migrants — mostly Syrian but also Afghan, Iranian and Iraqi, among others — have risked the 6-mile (10 km) sea crossing between Turkey and the Greek island of Lesvos. Fleeing war, homelessness, poverty and other struggles, they have been seeking a new life in northern Europe or North America.

Toward the end of 2015, European countries began to seal their borders, leaving the refugees and migrants trapped in Turkey and Greece. Over 100,000 still live in undersupplied camps like the main one on Lesvos. Called Mória, it is now home to some 20,000 people, which makes it the most crowded human settlement in the world.

Kanella was a real stray who briefly found a home in an unofficial camp created in the parking lot of a closed nightclub called OXY, just south of the beautiful town of Mólyvos (or Míthymna), Lesvos. The camp was run by volunteers, mainly from Europe and North America but also from some of the refugees' own countries. It was closed by authorities at the end of 2015.

I met Kanella while I was helping in the camp in the month before it was closed. I can't say for certain what became of her when her new home disappeared, though I know that several volunteers were hoping to adopt her. So I like to believe that — as in this story — she was lucky enough to find a home elsewhere.

May that be true for everyone who is searching.

STEVEN HEIGHTON is an award-winning author of poetry, novels and short stories. His work has been translated into twelve languages, and his most recent novel, *The Nightingale Won't Let You Sleep*, was published to rave reviews and has just been optioned for film. His most recent volume of poetry, *The Waking Comes Late*, won the Governor General's Literary Award for Poetry. He also reviews fiction for the *New York Times Book Review*, and he has taught and presented at universities and literary festivals around the world. *The Stray and the Strangers* is his first work for young readers. Steven lives in Kingston, Ontario.

MELISSA IWAI is an author and illustrator. She has illustrated over thirty books, including *Thirty Minutes Over Oregon* by Marc Tyler Nobleman, an Orbis Pictus Honor Book for Outstanding Nonfiction. Melissa lives in Brooklyn, New York.